LOTTIE LUNA

AND THE TWILIGHT PARTY

First published in Great Britain
by HarperCollins *Children's Books* in 2020
HarperCollins *Children's Books* is a division of HarperCollins*Publishers* Ltd,
HarperCollins Publishers
1 London Bridge Street
London SE1 9GF

The HarperCollins website address is
www.harpercollins.co.uk

1

ISBN 978–0–00–834301–9

A CIP catalogue record for this title is available from the British Library.

Printed and bound in England by CPI Group (UK) Ltd, Croydon CR0 4YY

MIX
Paper from
responsible sources
FSC www.fsc.org **FSC™ C007454**

This book is produced from independently certified FSC™ paper
to ensure responsible forest management.

For more information visit: www.harpercollins.co.uk/green

LOTTIE LUNA

AND THE TWILIGHT PARTY

VIVIAN FRENCH

Illustrated by Nathan Reed

HarperCollins *Children's Books*

ABOUT THE AUTHOR

VIVIAN FRENCH is the author of more than 300 books. In 2016 she was awarded an MBE for her services to literature, literacy, illustration and the arts, and in 2018 she received the Scottish Book Trust's Outstanding Achievement Award. She is the co-founder of the critically acclaimed Picture Hooks scheme to help emerging art graduates find their feet in the world of book illustration.

For the wonderful Aurelie Norman,

and all the children she inspires xxx

CHAPTER ONE

'**When** *the moon is blue*
Then we're all blue too . . .
And we'll all howl together
with a wowly wowly woo!'

Prince Boris, Lottie Luna's
big brother, was singing
at the top of his voice as
Lottie came hurrying into
the royal breakfast room.

'Boris, dear,' said Queen

Mila, 'MUST you sing that song?'

Boris made a face as Lottie sat down.

'You just don't appreciate modern music, Ma.'

'No, I don't think I do.' The queen cracked her boiled egg with a teaspoon. 'I prefer classical howling concerts.'

Lottie smiled at her mother. 'So you won't be buying a ticket to hear the Wonderful Werewolf Wailers?'

King Lupo came out from behind his newspaper. 'What's that, Lottie? Who's wailing? And where are they

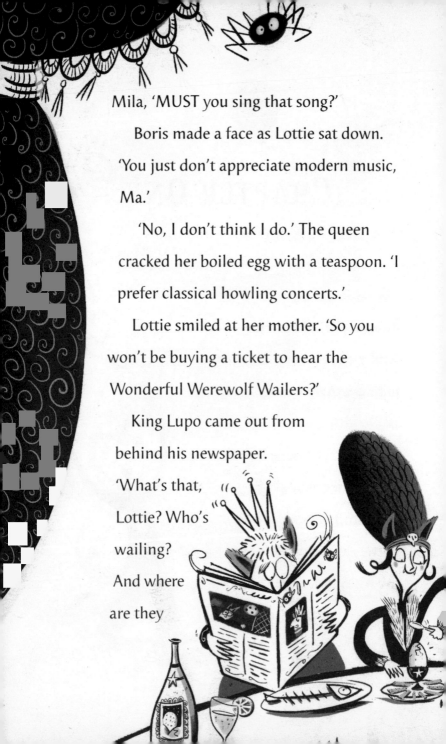

doing it?' He frowned. 'Not anywhere near me, I hope!'

Lottie giggled. 'It's okay, Pa. They're going to be wailing in the Pine Tree Grove next week, and that's miles away from here. It's going to be amazing! They don't just wail – they juggle and do acrobatics too!'

'Ahem.' The king cleared his throat. 'I hope you aren't thinking of going, Lottie. You must remember that you're a princess. Princesses should always be dignified, and jugglers and acrobats are NOT dignified.'

'Pa! Don't be so mean!' Lottie turned to her mother. 'Ma! I can go,

WOLF flakes

can't I? Boris is going – he got a ticket for free!'

'Huh! Well, you can't come with me,' Boris told her. 'My pal Volpin's brother plays guitar with them sometimes – that's how I got my ticket. And me and Volpin, we're going with all our friends. We don't want you tagging along.'

'That's SO not fair!' Lottie was about to explode, but the queen held up her hand.

'Lottie, dear – shouldn't you be on your way to school?'

Lottie looked at the clock, gasped and jumped to her feet. 'Oh, no! I'm going to be late!' And next minute she was rushing out of the door. Jaws, her bat, was dozing on the top of a picture; he woke up with a jump and flew after her, only just managing to whizz through the door before it shut.

As she ran down the path, Lottie was still thinking about the Wailers. 'I wonder if Marjory and Wilf would be interested in going?' she said to herself. 'What do you think, Jaws? I've never asked them what music they like . . . I'll ask them today. Maybe we could go together.' She gave a little skip. 'It's so lovely having new friends . . . I'm so lucky!'

Lottie had only been at Shadow Academy for a few weeks, but she was delighted with her new school – especially as, so far, nobody except her closest friends had discovered her secret.

Lottie was werewolf royalty. Not only that but she had been born during a lunar eclipse, which had given her special powers: she could run like the wind, she was exceptionally strong, she could hear almost as well as Jaws . . . and she could see

infinitely better than everyone else too. Round her neck was a moonstone necklace that celebrated her special birth; when she was happy, it glowed white, but if she was sad or worried it was dull . . . and, on the few occasions when Lottie was bored, it turned grey. Wilf and Marjory knew her secret, and they also knew her other secret – that she lived in Dracon Castle, her father was a king and her mother a queen.

'I just want to be ordinary,' Lottie had told them. 'So please don't tell anyone. Pa's only been king for six months . . . It's not like I was born a princess.'

'That's okay.' Marjory had grinned at her, and Wilf had winked.

'We won't say a word! We're friends, and friends always keep each other's secrets.'

'To the death!' Marjory had agreed, and they'd solemnly shaken hands.

Now, thinking about her friends, Lottie ran even faster – so fast that her little bat had trouble keeping up with her. 'Hurry up, Jaws!' she called. 'I've just had the most AMAZING idea, and I need to talk to Wilf. I think it might be Marjory's birthday soon . . . and, if it is, maybe we could take her to the Wailers concert for her birthday treat! Wouldn't that be perfect?'

Jaws was too puffed to do anything other than flap a wing.

Anyone else would have been late for school after such a late start, but Lottie's amazing speed meant she arrived in plenty of time. She flew through the entrance hall, hurtled down the corridor to her classroom and burst through the

15

door with a crash. Her teacher, Mrs Wilkolak, looked up and shook her head. 'Really, Lottie! MUST you arrive like a whirlwind?'

'Sorry, Mrs Wilkolak!' Lottie apologised. 'Please . . . do you know when Marjory's birthday is? Is it soon?'

Mrs Wilkolak picked up her register, and ran her finger down the names. 'It is indeed, Lottie. It's next week.'

'Oh, brilliant!' Lottie's eyes shone. 'Thank you! But please don't tell her I asked. I want to plan a surprise for her!'

Mrs Wilkolak smiled. 'What a lovely idea! Of course, I won't tell her.'

'Won't tell who what?' Wilf had come sauntering in and overheard Mrs Wilkolak.

'Wilf!' Lottie grabbed his arm, and pulled him into a corner. 'It's Marjory's birthday next week and I've got a fabulous idea for it – but I'm going to need your help!'

'Count me in,' Wilf said cheerfully. 'She deserves something nice. Her mum never gives her an actual party because money's a bit tight

in their house as she's got so many brothers and sisters. What's your idea?'

'Listen!' Lottie said, and she began to explain . . .

CHAPTER TWO

As Lottie and Wilf were talking, the rest of their classmates gradually arrived in the classroom, and Marjory came hurrying over to join her friends.

'Hi!' she said. 'You two look as if you're up to something! What's going on? Is it exciting?'

'Oh . . . nothing much. How was your weekend?' It was so obvious that Wilf was deliberately changing the subject that Marjory looked at him in surprise. Lottie saw Marjory's expression, and tried to make things better.

'We were talking about the Wonderful Werewolf Wailers,' she said. 'Do you like them?'

Marjory's face lit up. 'Oh, yes!' she said. 'I love them! And they're playing in the Pine Tree Grove next Sunday!' Her smile faded. 'But I can't possibly go. I've got to visit my gran that evening . . . and actually I wouldn't have been able to afford a ticket anyway. Are you two going?'

'I'd love to,' Lottie said, 'but I'm not sure if I can.' She gave Wilf a quick sideways glance, then asked Marjory, 'Why have you got to visit your

gran that evening? Couldn't you go the day after?'

Marjory shook her head. 'It's Gran's birthday, and we always go and visit her then. All the family come; we take a huge cake with enough candles for her, and for me as well. It's my birthday the day after, you see, so it's kind of a tradition that we celebrate together. I can't miss it.'

One of the other pupils had been listening to their conversation. Agatha Claws, a tall girl, leaned forward. 'I'm going to the Wailers concert,' she boasted. 'My father's taking me

and my cousin Kiki. Kiki's parents are moving house, so she's staying with us for a while, and the academy said she can come to school with us while she's here. She's the same age as me, and she loves the Wailers too. We're going to have front-row seats! They're VERY expensive, but my father says it doesn't matter.'

Lottie, Wilf and Marjory had always secretly called Agatha Awful Aggie; now they looked at her without enthusiasm. 'Good for you,' Lottie said.

'Yes.' Aggie smiled in a self-satisfied way. 'And did you know they do conjuring tricks as well as sing? And they ask for volunteers, and my father's going to make sure it's me they pick.'

'Oh.' Wilf shrugged, but before he could say anything else Mrs Wilkolak clapped her hands, and told them it was time for the register.

It was only as they went back to their places that
Lottie noticed that a new girl had come into
the class. She sat herself down close to Aggie,
and it was clear that they knew each other well.
That must be Aggie's cousin, Lottie thought, and
she looked at the girl with interest. She was like
Aggie, but her eyes were smaller, and closer
together . . . and she was staring round the
classroom as if she disapproved of everything and
everyone.

Mrs Wilkolak looked up from the register. 'You
must be Kiki Claws!' she said. 'You're Agatha's
cousin, aren't you? Welcome! We're delighted to
have you here at Shadow Academy for the next few
weeks. I expect Agatha's told you all about us.'

Kiki nodded, but she didn't return the teacher's friendly smile. 'Yes,' she said. 'It doesn't seem to be as much fun as my real school, though.'

Mrs Wilkolak raised her eyebrows. 'Well, give us time. This is a lovely class, as I'm sure you'll discover.'

Kiki nodded again, but didn't say anything. She turned away to whisper something to Aggie. Lottie's special powers meant that her hearing was extraordinarily acute, and she heard Aggie

whisper back, 'Lovely . . . well, except for Lottie Luna. She sometimes behaves as if she thinks she's cleverer than everyone else!'

Oh, no, Lottie thought as the new girl gave her a chilly stare. She sighed, and opened her history book.

They were studying famous werewolves that week, but even though Lottie loved history she found it hard to concentrate. She was still worrying about Marjory's birthday. *If Marjory's visiting her gran*, she thought, *there's no way we can take her to see the Wailers. We'll have to plan something else . . . but what?*

She was interrupted in her thoughts by Mrs Wilkolak asking her a question. 'So, Lottie . . . who was the most unusual werewolf king in the sixteenth century?'

Lottie had no idea. She blushed, and said, 'I'm really sorry, Mrs Wilkolak. I can't remember.'

Mrs Wilkolak frowned. 'A little more

25

concentration, please. Does anybody else know?'

Kiki put up her hand, and said, in a bored voice, 'Lupino the Second, because he lived to be a hundred and fifty years old. Everybody knows that. Except stupid people, of course.'

'Thank you, Kiki. And I should tell you that in Shadow Academy we don't call anyone stupid.' Mrs Wilkolak sounded cross, but Kiki just shrugged.

'Okay,' she said.

She's not very nice, Lottie thought to herself. *That was rude!*

The rest of the lesson seemed to drag. Lottie tried hard to keep her mind on the sixteenth century, but it was difficult. Her thoughts kept spiralling

away. Wilf had said that Marjory's mum never gave her a party, but did her family do something else instead for her? Lottie sighed, and decided she needed to have a private chat with Wilf at breaktime. She had thought the Wailers would be the perfect birthday treat . . . but now she could see that they'd need to come up with something else.

At breaktime Lottie looked for Wilf, but he was deep in conversation with another boy. It was Marjory who slipped her arm through Lottie's and said, 'What were you dreaming about this morning? You usually know more about werewolf history than any of us!'

'Oh, nothing really.' Lottie hoped she sounded convincing. 'Probably the Wonderful Werewolf Wailers.'

Marjory made a face. 'I do wish they were playing on my birthday instead of the day before. Wouldn't that be brilliant? We could all go together.'

'I thought you said you couldn't afford a ticket, Marjory!' Aggie and Kiki had come up behind the two girls, and Kiki gave Marjory a despising look. 'It must be horrid to be so poor. I'm glad I'm not.'

Lottie put her arm round her friend, and glared at Kiki. 'That's such a mean thing to say! I expect Marjory's glad she isn't you! I am! She'd never, ever say something like that!'

'Ooooh . . . temper, temper!' Kiki stuck her nose in the air. 'Come on, Aggie. Let's go and find someone nice to talk to.' And she pulled her cousin away.

Marjory stared after her. 'She's much worse

than Aggie,' she said. 'I'm so pleased you're my friend, Lottie. You and Wilf . . . we're best friends, aren't we?'

Lottie nodded. 'We certainly are.' She paused, and then asked, 'So don't you ever have a party on your birthday?'

'We do all the celebrating the day before, at Gran's house.' Marjory shrugged. 'There's not enough money for two parties. Sometimes we have a Family Howl on my actual birthday, and Mum always makes an extra cake – but we don't do anything else.' She saw Lottie was shocked, and added, 'It's okay. Really it is! I don't mind.'

'Come on, you two!' It was Wilf. 'Time for my favourite lesson . . . not! It's new-moon studies!' And he sped away.

Hmmm, Lottie thought as she walked back into

class. *When am I going to get to talk to him alone? We absolutely MUST organise a treat for Marjory . . . I know! If I don't get the chance to catch him at dinnertime, I'll write him a note! I just need some paper.* She fished in her pocket, and pulled out a picture of a rainbow that she had drawn the day before. *That'll do,* she told herself. *Wilf likes rainbows!*

CHAPTER THREE

Hi Wilf,

Could you meet me after school? I really, really,
REALLY need to talk to you about Marjory's
birthday! We need to plan a special surprise for her.
Love
Lottie

PS MAKE SURE MARJORY DOESN'T KNOW YOU'RE
MEETING ME! We don't want her guessing what
we're up to!

Lottie folded her note carefully, and wrote *WILF!* on the outside. It was the afternoon, and she still hadn't found Wilf on his own for long enough to talk to him; at lunch Marjory had been with them all the time, and Aggie and Kiki had been hanging around as well. Now Lottie was taking advantage of a couple of minutes between lessons; Mrs Wilkolak had gone out of the classroom to take the register to the head teacher, Madam Grubeloff, and everyone was meant to be reading.

Lottie tucked the note inside her copy of *Winnie, the Weirdest Werewolf Ever*, and jumped up from her seat. 'Here you are,' she said to Wilf. 'You said you wanted to borrow this when I'd finished it.' She handed him the book.

Wilf looked surprised. 'I never—' he began, but stopped as he saw Lottie wink at him. 'Oh, yes. Thank you!'

'Give it back when you've finished it,' Lottie said, and she sat back down again beside Aggie.

Aggie seemed to be concentrating very hard, but when Lottie wasn't looking she gave a little smile. She had seen Lottie writing the note, but she hadn't been able to read it; now she was dying to know what was going on. *I'll find out!*

she told herself. *Lottie's got a secret with Wilf . . . but what is it?*

Mrs Wilkolak came bustling back into the classroom just then. Everybody had to get their homework out, and Aggie kept a careful eye on Wilf as the class searched their school bags for the stories they had written the night before. She watched him reading Lottie's note and scribbling an answer, and she saw him tucking his reply in the book Lottie had given him. Pleased with herself, she nudged Kiki.

'Watch Wilf! He and Lottie have got a secret!' she whispered. 'They're passing notes to each other!'

'Aggie? Are you talking?' Mrs Wilkolak asked.

Aggie shook her head. 'I was just reading to myself, Mrs Wilkolak.'

'Then perhaps you'd like to read your story out loud,' the teacher said. 'I'm sure we'd all like to hear it!'

Aggie stood up and began to read. It was Kiki who saw the scrumpled piece of paper that was Lottie's note fall off Wilf's table. 'Oh, no!' she said loudly, 'I've dropped my pencil!' And jumping up, she slid across the classroom and snatched the note up before Wilf knew what was happening. Stuffing it in her pocket, she sat back down beside Aggie with a triumphant grin. 'Got it!' she hissed, but Aggie was in the middle of the most dramatic part of her story and didn't answer.

Lottie heard the whisper. *What's Kiki got?* she wondered, and she looked up to see what was going on – but Kiki was smiling innocently at

Aggie. All the same she was suspicious: Kiki had sounded much too pleased with herself.

I do wish she hadn't come to Shadow Academy, Lottie thought, *it was bad enough with Aggie, but now there's two of them . . .* And then she felt guilty. *Maybe she'll settle down,* she told herself. *She might get nicer. And she's only staying with Aggie . . . she won't be here forever.*

Wilf didn't find an opportunity to pass Lottie the book with his hidden note until just before the Evening Howl. It said that he'd be waiting for her after school, and she gave a sigh of relief. At last they'd be able to make a plan!

As she walked towards the Great Hall with Wilf and Marjory, Lottie was still trying to think of wonderful ideas for Marjory's birthday treat. She might not be able to make the concert, but

perhaps they could get the Wailers to play for her on her actual birthday? Why not? Boris knew one of the Wailers' brothers. Maybe she and Wilf and could find him, and ask him? She gave a little skip of excitement. Marjory looked at her in surprise, and Lottie smiled, but didn't explain.

The Evening Howl was as magical as always. The stars shone on the painted ceiling, and the tiny lights in the walls twinkled brightly. Madam Grubeloff swept on to the stage in a long black cloak trimmed with silver, and everyone was quiet as they waited for the Howl to begin. Aggie and Kiki were a little way in front of Lottie, and she was pleased to see that Kiki was looking impressed.

Madam Grubeloff held out her arms. 'Please

take your neighbour's hand in friendship,' she said. 'I'd like to begin by welcoming Kiki Claws to Shadow Academy! Kiki – we're delighted that you've joined us while you're staying with Agatha, and I hope you'll be very happy here.' She looked down at Kiki, who shuffled her feet but didn't say anything. Madam Grubeloff smiled

at her, and went on, 'And now let us begin our Evening Howl of peace and harmony.'

As the Howl began, Lottie held hands with Wilf and Marjory, and the glorious sound made her spine tingle. *Shadow Academy is the best school ever*, she thought to herself. *I'm so lucky to be here!* and she squeezed her friends' hands.

Once the Howl was over, Mrs Wilkolak led the class back to their room to collect their coats and bags, ready to go home. Kiki and Aggie were walking just ahead of Lottie, and they were whispering and giggling together; Lottie tried hard not to listen to what they were saying, but with her special powers she couldn't help overhearing when Aggie said, 'Will we show it to her today?'

Kiki's answer was a snigger. 'Let's wait until tomorrow morning. I want to teach that horrid Lottie Luna a lesson. I hate people who call me names!'

'Okay,' Aggie said, and then they began to walk faster and Lottie couldn't hear them any more.

'Oh, dear,' she said, and she rubbed her ears. It was difficult to know what to do. Nobody with

40

normal hearing could have heard Kiki . . . so should Lottie keep it to herself?

Before she could decide, she was back at the classroom. She picked up her school bag, called Jaws down from the picture rail where he'd been sleeping all day and hugged Marjory goodbye. 'See you tomorrow!' she said, and hurried out of school.

Aggie and Kiki watched her go.

'So – when do you think we should show the note to Mrs Wilkolak?' Aggie asked.

Kiki looked sly. 'Who said we were going to show it to Mrs Wilkolak?' She pulled the note out of her pocket, and tore it carefully. 'Look!'

Aggie looked.

MAKE SURE MARJORY DOESN'T KNOW YOU'RE MEETING ME! We don't want her –

'We'll show it to Marjory,' Kiki said, and her eyes were gleaming. 'She won't want to be Lottie's best friend once she reads that! I'll teach Lottie Luna what happens to people who tell me I'm mean.'

'I suppose so . . .' Aggie sounded doubtful, and Kiki stared at her.

'Aggie! Why are you standing up for Lottie?'

Aggie shrugged. 'She can be nice sometimes. I'd rather give the note to Mrs Wilkolak.'

'Too late,' Kiki said. 'I'm going to show it to Marjory tomorrow morning – and don't you dare say anything about me tearing a bit off or you'll be in trouble too!'

'Okay,' Aggie agreed. 'I promise.' Kiki gave her a sharp look, but said nothing.

CHAPTER FOUR

Wilf was waiting for Lottie outside the school gate. 'Hi!' he said, but he didn't sound as cheerful as usual, and Lottie looked at him in surprise.

'What's the matter?' she asked.

Wilf rubbed his nose apologetically. 'I'm really sorry – but I think Aggie's cousin might have found your note. I didn't notice at first that it had fallen off my table, and when I did it wasn't on the floor . . . and then I saw her reading something that looked a lot like it.'

Lottie made a face. So that was what Kiki and

Aggie had been talking about! 'Don't worry. I think they're planning to show it to Mrs Wilkolak, and get me into trouble. You know how she hates us passing notes!'

'Yes.' Wilf nodded. 'Sorry, Lottie. But what are we going to do about Marjory's party?'

'I was wondering,' Lottie said, 'if there was any chance we could ask the Wailers to play on her actual birthday?'

'Hmmm . . .' Wilf sounded unsure. 'How would we find them? And, even if we did, what would make them want to play at a kid's birthday party when they're used to performing to crowds?'

Lottie refused to be discouraged. 'We could at least ask,' she said. 'You never know. I'll ask my brother where we could look for them – he knows

someone who plays with them sometimes. Hey
– could you come home to tea with me today?
Then we can plan properly.' She grinned. 'You can
meet my weird family.'

'I'd need to tell my gran,' Wilf said. 'Could
Jaws take a message for me?'

Lottie nodded. 'Of course.'

As Jaws flew off
with Will's message, Lottie led
Wilf towards the path that led up to Dracon
Castle. As they hurried along, Lottie told him all
about her brother, and how Boris could be a bit
tricky sometimes.

Wilf laughed. 'Aren't big brothers always
tricky? Lottie – are you sure your parents won't

45

mind my coming to tea?'

Lottie shook her head. 'Ma will be really pleased to meet you.' She hesitated. 'And Pa . . . well, you'll have to excuse Pa. He does have a few airs and graces. He's got a bit grand since he became king. He's not—' She stopped, because Wilf was staring at her, his eyes popping out of his head. 'What's the matter?'

'I'd completely forgotten!' he said. 'Your dad's a king, and your mum's a queen!'

'Only since last year,' Lottie said. 'They were very ordinary before that. Look! Here's Jaws coming back!'

Lottie was right. Her little bat swooped down and landed on her shoulder. He was carrying a roll of paper, and she handed it to Wilf. 'This must be from your gran.'

Wilf read it, and laughed. 'She says she hopes my ears are clean, and I've got to be extra-specially polite!'

That made Lottie giggle. 'I don't think they'll check your ears. Come on . . . we're almost there!'

Wilf took a deep breath as they turned the last corner. He'd been expecting a wonderfully grand palace so he was surprised to see a rambling old building with dozens of crooked towers. There was ivy all over the walls, and several of the windows were almost covered.

'Welcome to Dracon Castle,' Lottie said. 'Come and meet Ma. She'll probably be in the kitchen. I'm sure there'll be something nice for tea . . . She's a very good cook. She worked in a café before she was made a queen; she gets very bored just cooking for us.'

As Lottie led Wilf under the big stone archway, he
began to feel nervous. The feeling got worse as
he followed Lottie in through a huge door, and
along a corridor. There were pictures hanging

on the walls, and he saw that they were kings
and queens, princes and princesses. They were
obviously very old; he even saw one that he
recognised from the history lesson they'd had

that morning. 'Wow! That's Lupino the Second! So is he one of your ancestors?'

Lottie shrugged. 'I suppose so. Well . . . a very distant one. Come on . . . the kitchen's this way!'

A door opened ahead of them, and a tall werewolf came towards them, eating a biscuit. 'Hello,' he said. 'I'm Boris.' He put the biscuit behind his back, clearly thinking it might make him look undignified. 'Prince Boris, actually. How do you do?'

Wilf had never met a prince before. He had read books about royalty, though, so he bowed low, and said, 'I'm Wilf, Your Majesty.' Boris looked pleased, but Lottie grabbed Wilf's arm. 'You don't need to do that,' she whispered. 'He's pleased enough with himself as it is. He wouldn't even be a prince if our incredibly ancient great-uncle hadn't died.' She made a face at her brother, and pulled Wilf towards the open door.

Wilf looked over his shoulder as he went. 'Excuse me, Your Majesty!'

'Don't! You'll make him worse!' Lottie hissed. And then they were in the kitchen.

Queen Mila was busy at the enormous old stove, and she didn't notice they were there until Lottie flung her arms round her mother's waist. 'Ma! Meet Wilf! Can he stay for tea?'

The queen smiled at Wilf, and wiped her hands on her apron. 'How do you do? I'm so pleased to meet you! Lottie says you're a very

51

special friend.' She looked around,
as if she was expecting someone
else. 'Isn't Marjory with you?
I thought you three did
everything together.'

'We're on a secret mission,' Lottie told her.
'Wilf and I want to plan a surprise party for
Marjory on her birthday, and we're going to try
and get the Wailers to play!'

'The Wailers?' Boris had come back into the

kitchen, and had heard what Lottie had said. 'At a kid's party? And how, exactly, do you think you're going to do that, little sister?'

Wilf was still a bit in awe of Boris. He bowed again, ignoring it when Lottie stuck an elbow in his ribs. 'Lottie said you knew someone and that you might be able to tell us where to find them, Your Majesty, so we can ask them.'

Boris raised a superior eyebrow, and tried to think of the most unlikely places to find the Wailers. 'She did, did she? Now, let me see . . . oh, yes. Holly Hollow. I'm almost sure you'll find them there. Or, if they aren't there, they might be at Four Oaks. Or even Heather Valley. They're rehearsing really hard at the moment. They're making sure that their concert is the best ever!'

Chapter Five

Wilf could hardly eat his tea, he was so excited. Boris didn't stay; he said he had things to do, and wandered away. 'Wow!' Wilf said. 'He's so cool! I wish I had a brother like that.'

'No you don't,' Lottie told him. 'He's really annoying and a terrible show-off.'

'Don't be unkind, Lottie,' Queen Mila said as she put a delicious-looking fruit cake on the table. 'Your brother was very helpful! He told you where to go to find your Moaners, didn't he?'

Lottie giggled. 'Wailers, Ma!'

'Oh, yes.' Her mother smiled. 'Wilf, dear, would you like some cake?'

But Wilf had eaten enough. 'Thank you very much, Your Majesty,' he said. 'That was delicious . . . but would it be all right if Lottie and I went to look for the Wailers now?'

Queen Mila glanced up at the clock. 'Just as long as Lottie's home by moonrise.'

As Wilf and Lottie walked away from Dracon Castle, Lottie patted his arm. 'Thanks, Wilf. If I'd asked if we could go out, Ma would probably have said no. Shall we start with Boris's first place – Holly Hollow? If we hurry, we might be able to check out Four Oaks as well.'

Wilf nodded, and Lottie began to run. She

hadn't gone far when she realised that Wilf was a long way behind; her special powers meant that it was too easy for her to outrun him. 'Oops,' she said, and stopped to wait for him. By the time he reached her, panting hard, she had had an idea. 'Wilf,' she said, 'suppose we split up? You go and look at Four Oaks, and I'll go to Holly Hollow . . . What do you think?'

Wilf was struggling to catch his breath, but he managed to nod. Lottie beamed at him. 'And, just supposing they aren't at either of those places, shall we go to Heather Valley tomorrow?'

'Okay.' Wilf was finally able to talk again. 'We can report back to each other at school in the morning.'

Lottie looked thoughtful. 'Maybe we should get there early to talk about it? Just in case Aggie and Kiki are about . . . and I don't want Marjory to suspect we're planning anything!'

'Good idea.' Wilf grinned at her. 'I think the Wailers will be at Holly Hollow, though! I just know it.'

'I do hope so,' Lottie said. 'But Boris can be really mean. He might have made it all up.'

'Really?' Wilf stared at her. 'But he's a prince!'

That made Lottie laugh out loud. 'He may be a prince, but that doesn't stop him from being ever so ordinary underneath. See you tomorrow!' And she began to run.

Wilf watched her vanish, and shook his head. *Nobody could catch her,* he thought. *Now . . . which is the best way to Four Oaks?*

Lottie, speeding towards Holly Hollow, was practising what she'd say to the Wailers. *I'm sure they'll want to help when they hear that Marjory's never, ever had a party,* she told herself. *I know I would!*

As she got closer, Lottie thought she could hear voices, and she ran even faster. *It's them!* she thought, but a moment later she realised

someone was singing 'Twinkle, Twinkle, Little Star'. *That can't be the Wailers!*

Lottie was right. As she slowed down to a walk, she saw that Holly Hollow was full of excited little cubs dancing in a circle. *Oops*, she thought.

The Wailers definitely aren't here. I'd better go home . . . and hope we can find them tomorrow.

CHAPTER SIX

Lottie was later than usual in setting off for school the following day. She had forgotten to do her homework the night before, and had had to rush through her maths while she was eating her toast, much to her mother's disapproval.

'Really, Lottie! You should have done your homework last night, instead of going out with Wilf. I know you wanted to start planning Marjory's birthday surprise, but your schoolwork should always come first. If I'd known you still had work to do, I'd never have agreed to you going out.'

Lottie waved her last piece of toast in the air.

'It's all right, Ma. I've done it now.' And with a whistle to Jaws she dashed out of the door.

As Lottie spun round the corner, Wilf was waiting outside Shadow Academy as he'd promised. She looked at him hopefully. 'Did you find the Wailers?' she asked, but Wilf just shook his head.

'Me neither,' Lottie told him. 'So, if Boris is right, then they must be at Heather Valley . . . Can

you come out again this evening?'

'As long as I'm not too late back.' Wilf grinned. 'My gran's ever so impressed I've been to tea at Dracon Castle!'

'*Shh!*' Lottie put her finger to her lips. 'I don't want everyone to know where I live!'

'Sorry,' Wilf apologised. 'I forgot.'

As soon as Lottie and Wilf reached the classroom, Lottie knew something was wrong. Marjory was in a corner, and Aggie and Kiki were whispering to her. She was looking really upset.

The next minute Marjory said loudly, 'I don't believe it!' and she marched away from the two girls.

'Are you okay?' Lottie asked. 'What were they saying to you?' And she glared at Kiki and Aggie.

For a moment, it seemed that Marjory was

going to tell her, but then she stopped and shrugged. 'It was nothing. They're just trying to be clever.'

'Are you sure?' Lottie put her arm round her friend. 'It looked as if they were being horrid to you.'

'No.' Marjory shook her head. 'It's fine.'

Kiki was watching from the other side of the classroom, and she nudged Aggie. 'Do you think Marjory believed us? That the note was real?'

'I don't see why not,' Aggie said. 'It was in Lottie's handwriting . . . and she looked ever so shocked when she read it.'

'She did, didn't she?' Kiki sniggered. Then she called out, 'Be careful, Marjory! Remember what we told you! Some people are ever so two-faced.'

Wilf frowned. 'Are you talking about Lottie?'

Kiki grinned at him, and it wasn't a friendly grin. 'Did I mention Lottie? I don't think I did. But you know her better than I do, so it's interesting that she's the first person you think of.'

'Lottie's never two-faced!' Marjory said indignantly, but Kiki shrugged.

'Time will tell.' She turned to Aggie. 'Did you do your maths homework last night?' And the two girls began to compare their answers.

Lottie, Wilf and Marjory spent the rest of the day together. Marjory was unusually quiet, but she still wouldn't tell Lottie and Wilf what Kiki and Aggie had said. 'It was nothing,' she told them, 'nothing at all.'

Lottie wasn't so sure. Her moonstone necklace was dull, so she knew something was very wrong ... but what?

Maybe they were teasing Marjory about never having a birthday party, she thought. *But they showed her something ... so what could it have been?*

She went on wondering, but for once she had

no bright ideas. *I'll ask Wilf later*, she thought. *He was sitting nearer than me.*

When school ended, Lottie gave Marjory an extra-special hug as she said goodbye, and Marjory looked pleased. 'We're best friends, aren't we?' she asked.

'Of course we are!' Lottie told her, and Wilf nodded his agreement. As Marjory ran off home, Lottie looked at her necklace to see if it was bright and gleaming again . . . but it wasn't.

'Wilf,' she said, 'what do you think Aggie and Kiki said to Marjory?'

Wilf shook his head. 'No idea.' He scratched his head. 'Could they have shown her the note you wrote me?'

'I don't think so,' Lottie said thoughtfully. 'That would have spoiled the surprise, but at the same time it would have made it clear we were planning something special for her. And surely that would make her happy – not sad.'

'True,' Wilf agreed. 'Oh, well. She did seem happier by the end of the day. Are we going to go to Heather Valley now?'

'Come home for tea first,' Lottie said, and the two of them ran off together.

CHAPTER SEVEN

When they reached Dracon Castle, Wilf didn't seem as nervous as he had been the day before. He said hello to the portraits in the corridor as if they were old friends, and managed to smile at Queen Mila. There was no sign of Boris; the queen said rather vaguely that she thought he was out at Holly Hollow with a friend.

But everything changed when King Lupo came stomping in for a cup of tea and a piece of cake. Wilf bowed very low indeed, and was too shy to answer any of the king's questions; Lottie had to answer for him.

'So, my lad, is Lottie treated like a proper princess at school?' King Lupo asked.

Wilf went scarlet, and mumbled something that the king couldn't hear.

'Eh? What was that? Speak up, lad!'

Lottie giggled. 'He said I'm treated like royalty, Pa.'

'Good, good. Glad to hear it. Now, where's my tea?' And King Lupo sat down and cut himself an enormous slice of fruit cake.

Lottie got up from the table, and beckoned to Wilf. 'We're going out now, Pa . . . We're going to try and find the Wailers. I'll be back very soon.'

'The Wailers? That dreadful band you told me about? Why do you need them?' King Lupo said.

'It's nothing, darling,' Queen Mila said soothingly, and she turned to Lottie. 'So you didn't find them last night, dear?'

'No.' Lottie shook her head. 'Hopefully they'll be at Heather Valley . . . unless Boris was trying to trick us.'

'Really, dear! I'm sure he wouldn't do that,' the queen said – but Lottie wasn't so certain.

It wasn't far to Heather Valley. Lottie kept to a gentle jog so Wilf was able to keep up with her,

and they chatted as they ran together along the long, winding path. Once they reached the hill above the valley, Lottie had to slow down even more; the hill was steep, and Wilf was puffing hard before they were even halfway up.

As they came closer, Lottie listened for sounds of music . . . but there was nothing. Her suspicions about Boris grew stronger and stronger as they climbed to the top, and when they stood looking down she wasn't surprised to see there was nothing there except for a rusty old truck.

'I knew it!' she said. 'Boris was playing games with us – OH!' She stopped mid-sentence. 'Wait a minute! There's someone down there . . .'

Lottie was right. A figure was climbing out of the truck and, even though they were a long way

away, Lottie, with her extra-keen eyesight, could see who it was. 'WOW!' she breathed. 'Wilf! LOOK!'

But Wilf had normal eyes, and all he could see was someone moving around.

Lottie was jumping up and down with excitement. 'Boris was right! It's Harper – the drummer from the Wailers! And he does juggling too! Oh, come on, Wilf . . . we have to talk to him!' And she set off at a run.

Wilf took a deep breath, and ran after her. He knew he'd never catch her, but he was determined not to be too far behind. He hurled himself down the slope and arrived, panting, just in time to hear Lottie say, 'So would you play at our friend's birthday party? Please? It would mean so much . . . She doesn't ever have a proper party.'

72

Harper was tall, with thick tortoiseshell glasses. He wasn't smiling, and Wilf began to feel anxious. Lottie had been so certain that they could persuade the Wailers to play for Marjory that he'd been carried along with her enthusiasm; now he began to have doubts.

'Play at a kid's party?' Harper was scornful. 'Why on earth would we want to do that?'

Lottie stood up straight. 'It would be very kind, and a good deed. And, if ever I can do anything for you, I certainly will.'

'You? But you're only a cub!' Harper began to laugh in a sneering kind of way. 'Are you joking? Now run along, and stop bothering me.'

Wilf took Lottie's arm. 'We'd better go, Lottie . . .'

But Lottie didn't move. She was gazing at another tall teenage werewolf who was walking round from the back of the truck. 'Froom!' she gasped. 'You're Froom, aren't you? The lead singer?'

Wilf was staring too. Froom was his hero, and he was so awestruck that he couldn't say a word.

'Hi, kids! You looking for autographs?' Froom grinned at the two of them. 'Not the best moment,

74

I'm afraid. Our truck's stuck in the mud . . . Loop has gone to get help.'

Harper made an unpleasant face at Lottie. 'See? We need proper help. Not silly kids hanging round, getting in the way.'

Lottie went closer to the truck. Froom was right; one of the back wheels had sunk into a deep muddy puddle, and Lottie looked at it thoughtfully. She was sure that with her special strength she could help . . . but would they believe her? Harper seemed like the kind of boy who thought girls were useless.

Lottie decided to pretend it would be her and Wilf together. 'We can help you push it out,' she said. 'Me and Wilf . . . we're very strong.' She gave Froom a sideways look. 'If we get your truck out, will you play at our friend's birthday party?'

Harper and Froom stared at her for a moment, and then Froom burst out laughing. 'It's a deal! I promise!' And he shook first Lottie's hand, then Wilf's, before slapping Harper on the back. 'Come on, Harper . . . let them have a go. Of course it won't work, but it'll give them something to talk about at school – "*The Wailers let us try and push them out of the mud!*" Good publicity!'

Harper shrugged. 'If you say so.' And he walked away from the truck and went to sit in the long grass. Froom sat down beside him, and the two of them began to discuss the next concert.

Lottie grabbed Wilf's arm, her eyes shining. 'Did you hear? They've promised they'll play at Marjory's party!'

Wilf was looking doubtful. 'But we haven't helped them yet,' he said. 'And it's ever such a big truck . . .'

'I can do it.' Lottie went to the back of the truck, and Wilf crossed his fingers in his pocket and followed her.

'Okay.' Lottie called on every ounce of the special powers that made her so unusually strong. 'One . . . two . . . three . . . PUSH!'

The truck lurched – and lurched again.

'Nearly,' Lottie panted, and she gave one final

push – and it was free.

'WOWSERS!' Froom's mouth dropped
open in astonishment. 'What kind of kids
ARE you?'

Wilf shook his head. 'It was Lottie, not me,' he said, but Froom and Harper hardly heard him.

They were on their feet, staring at the truck.

'You kids are AMAZING! We'll be on time for our next gig now . . . and it's all thanks to you!'

Lottie went to stand in front of them. 'So you'll

play at our friend's birthday party? It's the day after your concert . . . and the party's going to be in Silver Grove!'

'What?' Harper looked horrified. 'Us? Play at a kid's party?'

Lottie nodded. 'You promised!' She turned to Froom. 'You did, didn't you?'

There was a pause, and then Froom said, 'Yes. I did. We'll play at your friend's party.' He shook his head. 'I never, ever thought I'd hear myself say that . . . but a promise is a promise.'

'But—' Harper was obviously going to argue, and Froom held up his hand. 'It's okay, Harper. I gave my word.' He suddenly smiled. 'Might be fun! It's ages since I went to a birthday party! Tell you what, kid – we'll play the birthday girl a special song. Might even magic up a little

surprise for her! What's her name?'

Lottie's eyes were sparkling. 'Marjory! And that's Wilf, and I'm Lottie Luna! Thank you so, so, SO much!'

'No problem, kid.' Froom patted her shoulder. 'Come on, Harper! Let's hit the road!'

And the two tall Wailers swung into their truck and roared away, leaving Lottie and Wilf looking after them with the hugest smiles.

CHAPTER EIGHT

Lottie danced along the path to Shadow Academy the following morning, while Jaws flew in circles over her head. 'Everything's going brilliantly well, Jaws! All Wilf and I have to do now is to ask Marjory if she'd like to come to tea on her birthday . . . and then we can give her the best

surprise ever!' Lottie spun round in excitement.
'And we'll invite the rest of the class too. We'll
have a Twilight Party in Silver Grove . . . but
we won't tell anyone about the Wailers. It'll be
amazing! And I'll ask Ma to make a super-extra-
special birthday cake, and little sausage rolls, and
pizza, and sandwiches . . . Oh, it's going to be just
perfect!'

She twirled again, and as she did so she
noticed her little moonstone necklace was
looking dull. She stopped dancing, and stood still.

'Why isn't it glowing? Nothing's wrong . . . At
least, I don't think it is.' She gave the moonstone
a little rub with her finger, but it made no
difference. *That's so weird*, she thought. *I wonder
what it can be? Everything's going so well!*

Lottie and Wilf had made a plan to ask

Marjory out for her birthday tea before the start of lessons, but she had arrived at the last moment, so there hadn't been time yet. Still, Lottie had smiled at her as she came in, and Marjory had smiled back . . . although it wasn't her usual cheerful grin.

Kiki saw her smile at Lottie, and made a nasty snorting noise. 'So you still want to be friends with Lottie, Marjory? I'd hate to be friends with someone who didn't want me . . . but then the people I know don't write nasty notes to their friends.'

Lottie swung round and stared at Kiki. 'What do you mean?' she asked.

Kiki stuck her nose in the air. 'I wasn't talking to you, Lottie Luna!'

'*Shh*, Kiki!' Aggie said. 'Here comes Mrs Wilkolak.'

Aggie was right. The teacher came bustling into the classroom, carrying a pile of paper.

'Good morning, everyone! We've got a special treat today! We're going to create portraits of all the werewolf kings and queens we read about in our lesson yesterday, and we'll make a mural outside in the corridor.'

Wilf giggled. 'Hey! That'll end up looking just like the corridor in Dracon Castle—' He stopped, and put a hand to his mouth as he realised what he had said. Only Lottie and Marjory had heard

him, but they were both staring at him – and Marjory's eyes were full of tears.

Lottie was horrified. It was all too obvious that Marjory had realised that Wilf had been to Lottie's home without her, even though it wasn't like that at all . . . and the next minute Marjory gave a little sob and went flying out of the classroom.

'Oh, no! Marjory thinks that I've invited you to tea, and I didn't ask her too!' Lottie was pale with remorse. 'That's so awful! I'm going to have to think of an explanation . . . but I can't tell her the real reason you came, or it'll spoil the surprise.'

'Wilf! Lottie! Are you talking?' Mrs Wilkolak was peering over her spectacles. She had been so engrossed in writing on the whiteboard, with her back turned to the class, that she hadn't noticed Marjory slip out.

'Sorry,' Wilf said. 'I . . . I was just saying what a great idea that was.'

Mrs Wilkolak gave him a stern look. 'I'm glad you think so – but please don't talk in class.'

'Please, Mrs Wilkolak, Marjory's run—' Kiki began, but she didn't finish her sentence. Mrs Wilkolak was frowning at her. 'I said no talking!' And she looked so fierce that even Kiki was quiet.

The rest of the morning dragged. At breaktime Lottie couldn't find Marjory, and neither could

Wilf, and she had disappeared at lunchtime too. When the afternoon lessons began, she came in late, and her eyes were very red, as if she'd been crying. Lottie wanted to run and hug her, but she didn't dare. Mrs Wilkolak was in one of her fiercest moods.

I'm going to talk to her after school, Lottie told herself. *Even if she tries to run home as soon as the bell goes, I'll catch her . . . She has to tell me what's going on! Kiki and Aggie definitely did something that upset her yesterday . . . and it looks like now me and Wilf have too. But she and me and Wilf are best friends, and friends tell each other when things go wrong!*

But this plan didn't work either. When it was time for the Evening Howl, Marjory was nowhere to be seen. Somewhere between the classroom

and the Great Hall she had vanished; Lottie and Wilf looked everywhere, but there was no sign of her.

As soon as the Howl was over, Lottie and Wilf rushed to ask Mrs Wilkolak if she knew what had happened to their friend.

'She's missing!' Lottie said. 'And we're really worried about her.'

Mrs Wilkolak peered over the top of her spectacles. 'You don't need to worry,' she said. 'Marjory's gone home early. She said she wasn't feeling at all well, so we called her mother to come and collect her.'

Lottie and Wilf looked at each other as Mrs Wilkolak picked up her bag and walked towards the staffroom. 'That's it,' Lottie said, and she banged her fist on the table. 'I'm going to ask Kiki

89

and Aggie what they showed her! It must have been something really, REALLY horrible.'

Wilf nodded. 'I'll come with you,' he said, but when they got back to the classroom Aggie and Kiki were gone.

Lottie sank down on a chair with a groan. 'Oh, Wilf!' she said. 'I was so happy this morning, and now everything's gone wrong! We absolutely have to talk to Aggie and Kiki tomorrow.'

'Or we could call round at Marjory's house,' Wilf suggested, and Lottie sat up and looked hopeful.

'That's a brilliant idea,' she said. 'Why didn't I think of that? Can we go now?'

Wilf nodded. 'I'll get my coat.'

Lottie and Wilf were quiet as they hurried towards Marjory's home. It didn't take them very long; she lived much nearer to Shadow Academy than Lottie, up a quiet, tree-lined road.

'Have you been here before?' Lottie asked, and Wilf nodded.

'Just a couple of times. Marjory's mum's nice, but she's so busy with the little ones that she doesn't really like having extra kids around.' He grinned. 'You'll have to come and have tea with my gran one day. She absolutely loves company!'

'I'd like that,' Lottie said. Then, 'Is that Marjory's house?'

'That's it,' Wilf said.

Marjory lived in a small cottage, and the garden outside was criss-crossed with washing lines hung with clothes of every size. As they

got closer, they saw a couple of little werewolf
cubs playing in the garden, and Wilf gave them
a wave. 'That's Gigg and Fizz,' he told Lottie.
'They're twins.'

Lottie grinned at the little cubs, but they just
stared at her with big round eyes.

'Hi there! Can you tell Marjory we've come to
see her?' Wilf asked.

'She don't want to see nobody.' One of the twins frowned.

'They was nasty to her at school,' the other one said. 'It made her cry!' And then they ran inside, slamming the door behind them.

'Oh, dear.' Wilf stared at the closed front door. 'Who do you think they mean? And what do we do now?'

Lottie was thinking. 'We write her a proper invitation to come out to tea on her birthday . . . and we tell her how much we miss her. I'll write an invitation tonight . . . a really special one.' A fierce expression settled on her face. 'I know this is all Kiki's fault, and tomorrow I'm going to tell her what I think of her!' She clenched her fists. 'The three of us were all so happy before she came to Shadow Academy . . . Why did she have to come?'

93

Wilf shrugged. 'Who knows? She's making Aggie worse too. I mean, Aggie's not one of my favourite people, but she was okay sometimes.'

Lottie sighed. 'I know. I was really getting used to her.' She paused for a moment. 'Wilf . . . suppose we get Aggie on her own, and ask her what was in the paper she and Kiki showed Marjory? She might tell us.'

'Maybe.' Wilf sounded doubtful. 'We could try.'

'I can't think of anything else to do,' Lottie said gloomily. She was trying as hard as she could not to listen to the voices inside the cottage. She was almost certain that she had heard Marjory say that she never wanted to go to school again, and it was making her feel terrible.

CHAPTER NINE

Lottie tried to write Marjory an invitation that evening. She found a piece of card, and all her favourite coloured pencils, but she couldn't think of the best way to say all the things she wanted to say. Should she mention Kiki and Aggie? Should she ask Marjory what had upset her so much?

Her moonstone necklace was still grey and dull, and that made her feel dull as well. In the end she wrote:

AN INVITATION TO OUR
VERY BEST FRIEND, MARJORY!
PLEASE COME TO A TWILIGHT PARTY
IN SILVER GROVE ON YOUR BIRTHDAY
WITH LOTS OF LOVE FROM
LOTTIE AND WILF

I hope that's all right, Lottie thought. *I'll show Wilf in the morning . . . and if Marjory's at school we can give it to her.*

She looked at the invitation, and drew a couple more hearts on it, and some extra flowers. *And we'll have to think of the best way to ask the rest of the class to come to the party without Marjory knowing.*

She put her pencil down, and stared into

space while she thought about it. *There's no point in inviting them yet, just in case Marjory says she doesn't want to come. Oh, dear . . . I do so wish I knew what's gone wrong!*

She went to look for an envelope, and as she was hunting in her cupboard she had an idea. 'Why don't I take the invitation round to her house now? It wouldn't take me long. And perhaps it would cheer Marjory up, and then she'll want to come to school tomorrow!'

The idea of being able to do something positive made Lottie feel much happier. She put the note in an envelope, wrote *MARJORY* on the front, and ran to tell her mother she was going out.

'Again?' the queen asked.

'It's all to do with Marjory's surprise birthday party,' Lottie told her. 'And, Ma . . . if we can

arrange it, do you think you could make her a cake? A really special one?'

'Of course, dear.' Queen Mila looked pleased. 'And sandwiches and buns and biscuits?' She clapped her hands. 'And sausages and burgers and pizza! Oh, what fun! I haven't cooked properly for ages.'

'Thank you!' Lottie gave her mother an enthusiastic hug. 'You're the best!' And then she was out of the door and running to deliver the invitation. Down the path she sped, in and out of the trees, and the owls flapped their wings in astonishment.

The road to Marjory's cottage was on the other side of Shadow Academy, and Lottie slowed down a little as she passed her school. There were lights on in the windows, and she wondered what was happening.

Maybe it's being burgled! she thought.

Anxious to see what was going on, she swung herself up into the branches of a tree so she could peer in – and was disappointed to find it was only the cleaners. Lottie watched for a moment as they swept and mopped the floors, and emptied the waste-paper bins into big brown sacks. *That's our classroom*, she thought. *Goodness! We didn't clear up very well after making our pictures today. I'm surprised Mrs Wilkolak didn't tell us off!*

One of the cleaners was talking to another, and Lottie was just about to slide down her tree

when something caught her eye. The cleaner
was looking at a piece of paper . . . and Lottie
recognised it. It was her rainbow picture; the
picture she had written her note on. Lottie leaned
forward to see more clearly – but even as she
watched the picture was dropped into a brown
sack, and was gone.

So it was in the waste-paper basket, she thought
as she jumped down . . . and, as she landed, the
jolt made a wild idea pop into her head. *If I can
find that note, Wilf and I can show it to Marjory –
and then she'll know exactly why Wilf came to tea
and we left her out!*

Not quite daring to march into Shadow
Academy, Lottie lurked outside in the darkness
under the trees until the cleaners started bringing
out the rubbish sacks. They were stacked up by

the dustbins, and Lottie suddenly realised she had no idea which sack was the one she wanted ... but she refused to be defeated. *I can show her the note with her invitation*, she thought, *and then everything will be all right again!*

The cleaners seemed to take forever to finish their work, but at last they put the final sack down, and left. The lights went out in the school, and everything was very quiet as Lottie tiptoed towards the bins.

I'm just going to have to look in them all, she thought – but it wasn't quite as difficult as she had feared. It was immediately obvious which was the rubbish from the baby class, and also from the top class. *Scary*, Lottie thought as she looked at the complicated moon-cycle tests. *I'm sure I'll never understand those!*

The next sack was easy too; Lottie recognised the diagrams as being from the form below hers, and put it to one side. Only two were left, and she dived into the first with enthusiasm.

It was lucky that Lottie's eyesight was unusually good. She was able to check out paper after paper, even though the light was dim . . . but there were so many scraps! By the time she got to the bottom of the sack, she was almost ready to give up. Only the thought of Marjory kept her going.

She picked up the last sack with a sigh. *What if it isn't in here after all?* she thought. *I've already spent loads of time looking. Ma will be worrying about me.* She opened the sack, plunged in her hand . . . and pulled out the rainbow picture.

'Oh!' Lottie stared at the paper. 'It's been

103

torn in half . . . WAIT A MINUTE!' She looked more closely. 'But it's not just been torn any old how . . . someone's torn it really carefully . . . But who, and why?' She shut her eyes, and tried to remember what she'd written to Wilf.

'I know I told him to make sure Marjory didn't know we were going to meet each other, because we didn't want her guessing what we were planning.'

Lottie froze. 'That's it!' She snatched up the paper and peered at it. 'Yes, yes, YES! It still says, "guessing what we're up to"!' She sat back on her heels while all kind of thoughts whirled round in her head . . . and settled into a certainty.

'Kiki and Aggie must have shown Marjory the note! But only the bit that said "we don't want her" . . . Of course she was upset! But what do I do now?' Lottie glanced up at the sky. 'Oh, no . . . it's getting ever so late . . . but I have to see Marjory first! I absolutely have to!'

And she jumped to her feet, carefully tucked the remains of the rainbow picture into her pocket and began to run. She ran so fast that

a couple of rabbits, busy nibbling grass, were caught by surprise and fell over, squeaking indignantly. Lottie didn't stop. Her feet hardly touched the ground as she sped along the tree-lined road, and she only slowed when she reached Marjory's front gate. Pausing for a second to catch her breath, she ran up the path and knocked at the door.

At first there was no answer, although Lottie could hear the sound of movement inside the house. Then, just as she was beginning to think nobody was going to open the door, there was a shout, 'Marjory! The boys are in the bath! Go and see who's there!'

And a moment later Marjory was standing in the doorway. She gave a little gulp when she saw Lottie, as if she was trying not to cry.

Lottie grabbed her hands. 'Marjory – you've

got to tell me! Did Kiki and Aggie give you a message? A message saying me and Wilf didn't want you?'

Marjory stared at her in astonishment, then nodded. 'They showed me. They didn't give it to me. They showed me what you had said.'

'I thought so! Oh, Marjory – we'd NEVER not want you! That was only a bit of the message! Please, PLEASE come to school tomorrow! But I've got to go now, or Ma will be FURIOUS!'

And then she was gone.

CHAPTER TEN

Lottie woke up early the next morning, wondering if she had made a terrible mistake. What if – Lottie could hardly bear to think about it – Marjory hadn't believed her, and never wanted to be her friend again?

'What do you think, Jaws?' She peered at her little bat, but he was still asleep. Lottie sighed. 'Well . . . there's only one way to find out.'

An hour later, she was on her way to Shadow

Academy. She didn't run as fast as usual, and she hadn't dared to look at her moonstone necklace. She went steadily down the path, and was surprised to see Wilf coming towards her.

'Hi!' he said. 'I came to meet you . . . Did you make Marjory an invitation?'

'OH!' Lottie nearly dropped her school bag. 'I forgot! I forgot to give it to her!'

She couldn't believe how silly she'd been. She'd been so busy hunting through the bins at school and looking for the note that she'd forgotten to do the very thing she'd set out to do.

'Give it to her?' Wilf raised his eyebrows. 'Did you see her?'

Lottie nodded. 'Yes. I went to take the invitation round to her, but then on the way I made a HUGE discovery – and so I forgot to give

it to her.' And as they walked towards Shadow
Academy she told him her adventures of the
evening before. Wilf listened in silence, but as she
finished he whistled.

'WOW! What do we do now?'

'I told Marjory about the note being torn,'
Lottie said, 'but I don't know if she entirely
believed me. Besides, Kiki and Aggie can't get
away with being so mean. We've got to make
them own up.'

Wilf blinked. He had never seen Lottie look so
determined.

Marjory wasn't in the classroom when Lottie and
Wilf walked in. Kiki and Aggie were chatting in
a corner, and Kiki looked up with a sneer. 'Oh,

look! It's the wonderful Lottie Luna! Little Miss
Perfect!'

Lottie took no notice. She was watching the
door; two boys were the next to come in, and
Lottie's heart missed a beat. Maybe Marjory was
going to stay at home! Then another girl arrived,
and her friend was right behind her.

'No Marjory today, I see,' Kiki said loudly, but
even as she spoke the door opened a fourth time
and Marjory walked in.

'Ooooooh! Here she is at last,' Kiki began to
sneer, but before she could say anything more
Lottie was standing in front of her, eyes blazing.

'You took my message to Wilf, and you used
it to hurt Marjory, didn't you?' She pulled the
rainbow note from her pocket, and waved it
under Kiki's nose. 'Where's the piece you tore

out? The piece you showed Marjory? The piece that said we didn't want her!'

Kiki shrugged. 'I don't know what you're talking about.' She turned to Aggie. 'We've never seen any note from the perfect Lottie Luna, have we?'

'Yes, you have!' It was Wilf. 'I saw you pick it up when it fell off my desk!'

Kiki's eyes narrowed. 'I never picked anything up. What would I want with your stupid notes? I don't care if you're planning special surprise birthday parties! Why would I?'

Lottie gave a triumphant snort. 'So how do you know that was what we were planning if you didn't read the note?'

For a moment, Kiki tried her best to look as if she didn't understand what Lottie had said, but then, with a terrible scowl, she jumped to her feet and picked up her school bag. 'I'm leaving! I never wanted to come to this stupid school anyway . . . I hate it! I'm going to make Father let me go home. Come on, Aggie!'

But Aggie didn't move. 'I'm not coming.'

Kiki glared at her, then swung her school bag on to her shoulder and stormed out of the classroom. As she left, Aggie looked at Lottie, and there were tears in her eyes.

'I'm sorry, Lottie. We did find the note, and I wanted to show Mrs Wilkolak so you got into trouble . . . but Kiki tore it and made me promise not to tell.' Aggie rubbed her arm. 'She pinched me loads . . . She's my cousin, but I don't like her. Not at all. And I'm really, really sorry.' She gulped. 'You can have my ticket for the Wailers concert to make up for it.'

Lottie stood very still, and then she astonished Aggie by hugging her. 'That's the nicest thing you've ever, ever said, Aggie Claws! Thank you, but I won't take your ticket. I wouldn't want to leave Marjory and Wilf out. But there's

something I want to say . . .'

She turned to the class, and held out her arms.

'You're all invited to Marjory's birthday party next Monday! Please come to Silver Grove at twilight . . . It's going to be the best party ever, and there'll be the most AMAZING surprise!' She saw Aggie's face, and added, 'You too, Aggie! EVERYONE'S invited . . . except Kiki!'

CHAPTER ELEVEN

And it was the best party ever . . .

Lottie and Wilf spent all day Sunday helping Queen Mila cook all kinds of delicious party foods, and even Boris came to lend a hand in the afternoon.

'Don't you need to get ready for the Wonderful Werewolf Wailers concert tonight?' Wilf asked him, but Boris shook his head, and winked at him.

'I'm not going tonight. My friend's brother – the one whose brother is a Wailer – told me a secret. I'm going to go to Silver Grove tomorrow! That's going to be loads more fun!'

Lottie stopped cutting out biscuits and stared at him. 'Who said you were invited? It's a party for Marjory!'

For once, Boris was taken aback. 'Oh. Oh, yes. I didn't think.' He gave Lottie a hopeful look. 'I can come, can't I?'

'Hmmm . . . what do you think, Wilf?' Lottie put her hands on her hips. 'Does my brother deserve to come?'

'Well . . . we'd never have found the Wailers if he hadn't told us where they were rehearsing,' Wilf said, and Lottie grinned.

'Hmmm. I suppose you're right.' Lottie hesitated for a moment, and scratched her head. Then she turned to her brother. 'Okay, Boris! You are hereby invited to Marjory's party!'

'Phew.' Boris grinned at Wilf. 'Thanks.' He pointed to the window. 'And I think tomorrow's going to be MUCH the best day to see them . . . look! It's absolutely tipping down with rain!'

Boris was right. The weather was terrible; winds were whipping at the trees, and the rain was torrential. 'Oh, dear,' Lottie said. 'Do you think it'll be okay for tomorrow?'

The queen nodded. 'It's supposed to be a lovely day.'

Queen Mila, a little to her own surprise, was
quite right. The following morning the sun was
shining as Lottie hurried to school, and by the
time she, Marjory and Wilf went home again the
weather was glorious.

They had agreed to meet in Silver Grove just before twilight, and all day Marjory was glowing with excitement. 'I can't believe you've arranged a party for me,' she kept saying, and each time Lottie and Wilf chuckled to themselves as they thought of the surprise to come.

Aggie was very quiet in school; she said her father had taken her home early from the concert because it was so wet, and she kept sneezing. Wilf asked her if Kiki was still staying with her, and she shook her head. 'She made her father take her home. She said she hated Shadow Academy, and she hated me too . . . and I'm glad she's gone!'

As twilight drew nearer, Lottie grew more and more excited. She and Wilf had hung candle lanterns in the trees, and Boris had helped them carry the baskets of food and drink.

'It looks SO wonderful!' Lottie said as she lit the last lantern. 'A magic twilight party!'

All the guests thought so too. There were oohs and aahs from everyone as they arrived, especially Marjory.

Hardly had they sat down when there was the sound of music . . . and all three of the Wonderful Werewolf Wailers arrived, bounding into the centre of the grove, playing their guitars as they came.

'*OOOOOOOOOOOH!*' Marjory's shriek of delight made Lottie and Wilf look at each other with enormous smiles. 'You two are the BEST EVER!' Marjory told them, and she was glowing with excitement. 'I can't believe it! It's the Wailers! And they're here on my birthday!'

Froom was in the lead, and as soon as he saw

Lottie he put his guitar down and began to juggle
. . . and Harper and Loop tumbled over each
other, faster and faster, until they were just a blur.
Then they snatched up their guitars again, and
began to play. 'Come on, everyone!' Froom called.
'Let's see you dance! This isn't a concert . . . this is
a party! It's time for fun!'

THE WAILERS

On and on went the music, until even Lottie was breathless from dancing. At last, as the twilight deepened into dusk, the tunes slowed.

'Everyone sit down,' Froom ordered. 'We've got a special song we've never played before, and we want to know what you think of it.'

Lottie and her friends did as they were told . . . and Froom began to sing.

'If you think you're lonely, and the world is at an end,

Here's a way to beat the blues . . . just find a loyal friend.

Friends will always comfort you,

Friends will raise a smile.

When you want a helping hand,

They'll go the extra mile—

'And now all together for the chorus!' he shouted.

'A friend in need

Is a friend indeed!'

Froom beckoned to Marjory.

'So . . . let's have three cheers for the birthday girl!'

Everyone cheered loudly, and as the noise died

away Marjory looked at Lottie. 'How did you do it?' she asked. 'How on earth did you get the Wailers here?'

Lottie grinned. 'It's a long story. We'll tell you later. But now – it's time for food.' She smiled at the Wailers. 'Would you like to join us?'

'Try and stop us,' Froom said cheerfully. 'We're starving!'

After all the dancing, everyone was hungry – and the food disappeared at speed.

When it was finally time for the cake, Lottie went to fetch it from where she had hidden it under a tree.

Froom saw what she was doing, and whispered to Harper, and Harper whispered to Loop . . . and

as Lottie carried the cake into the middle of the
party they began to play 'Happy Birthday to You!'

Marjory looked at Lottie and Wilf. 'Thank you!' she said. 'It's the best birthday party anyone ever had!'

And, as she hugged her friends, Lottie saw that her moonstone necklace was shining as brightly as the stars in the dark night sky above.

LOOK OUT FOR ANOTHER LOTTIE ADVENTURE!

TURN THE PAGE FOR AN EXTRACT . . .

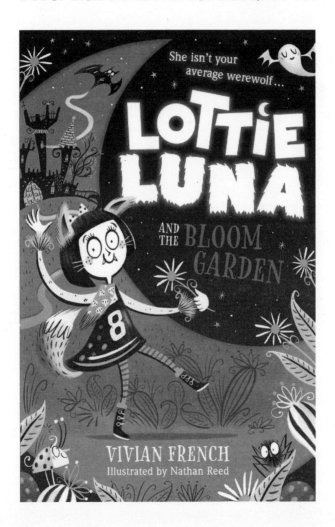

CHAPTER ONE

Plop!

King Lupo jumped and looked up at the ceiling.
Water was oozing through a zigzag crack and
splashing on his head.

'I did warn you, dear,' said Queen Mila. 'If you will insist on sitting at the head of the table, you'll get dripped on.' She passed the king a napkin and he wiped his ears.

'A king should always be kingly,' he announced. 'I may not have been king for long, but I do know how to behave. A king is head of his people, so he should sit at the head of the table – drips or no drips! And talking about behaving, 'WHERE is Lottie? She's late for breakfast!'

'I think she's getting ready,' Queen Mila told him. 'Do remember, dear – it's her first day at her new school, so she's bound to be a little nervous.'

'Nervous? Why would she be nervous?' King Lupo dodged another drip and took a bite of his toast. Finding it was soggy, he made a face and put it back on his plate.

Queen Mila sighed. 'You know how happy she was at her last school, dear. She had lots of friends and was popular with the teachers too. She doesn't know anyone at Shadow Academy. She's starting all over again.'

'But she's the daughter of a king now!' Lupo raised his whiskery eyebrows. 'She'll find that she's treated with the greatest respect!'

'I don't think—' Queen Mila had been about to say that she didn't think that would make any difference, but she was interrupted by the door being flung open with a crash, and Lottie appeared. She was clutching her school bag in one hand and a bunch of pencils in the other, which she waved wildly at her mother.

'Ma! I can't find my pencil sharpener anywhere. It's hopeless! Ever since we moved, everything's been upside down. Nothing's where it should be – *and* there are ZILLIONS of spiders in the bathroom! Do we have to live here?'

Boris, Lottie's older brother, stopped admiring himself in the cracked old mirror by the fireplace and joined in. 'But we're royalty now, Lottie! Pa's a king, and kings live in castles – even if they are a bit crumbly and falling down.'

'Well said, Boris my lad!' King Lupo beamed at his son. 'Dracon Castle is our home. I'm sure once we've done a few repairs we'll be extremely comfortable here. Now, Lottie, sit down and eat your breakfast.'

'Hmmmph . . .' Lottie sighed thoughtfully as she remembered her old home. Although it had been small and cramped, it had been warm and very cosy. The castle they had inherited had so many rooms she couldn't count them all, and every single one was freezing cold.

'I'm not hungry,' she said. 'Honestly, Pa,

I couldn't eat a thing.' She looked at her mother. 'Ma – do you think it'll be okay at Shadow Academy? It's awful being new in the middle of a term.'

Her mother hugged her. 'I'm sure you'll make lots of friends in no time at all.'

'Huh!' Boris looked down his nose. 'Who'd want to be friends with her? Not me!'

Lottie made a face at him, then stuffed her blunt pencils into her bag. 'I'll be off now,' she said. 'I don't want to be late, not on my first day. See you later, darling Ma. Remember I won't be back until after moonrise! Bye, Pa!' And she whisked out of the dining hall, banging the door behind her. Jaws, her pet bat, was waiting for her on the other side, and together they hurried along the cold, dark corridor. With a heave and a tug, Lottie managed to open the creaking front door . . . and then they were out in the morning sunshine.

As Lottie ran down the long, winding path that led from Dracon Castle to the village below, she was already worrying about the day ahead. 'It's all very well Ma saying I'll make friends, Jaws, but what if I don't? They'll probably hate me because Pa's the new king, and they'll think I'm all posh and stuck-up when I'm not. But . . .' An idea popped into her head, and she stopped to think about it. 'What if I don't tell anyone I live in a castle? Or that Pa's a king? I'll say I'm plain Lottie Luna and that I'm really rather ordinary, just like everyone else.'

Liking the idea, she walked slowly on. 'But what about my superpowers? Can I hide them too?' She touched the little moonstone necklace that she always wore and then, with a decisive nod, tucked it under her jumper. 'There! It's gone.' And with a skip and a jump she was on her way.

If anyone had watched Lottie running along, they would have easily guessed that she wasn't the ordinary little werewolf she so badly wanted to be. Born on the night of a lunar eclipse, when the moon was full, she had been gifted with special powers. She could run like the wind, her eyesight was as sharp as an eagle's, and she was far stronger than her older brother . . . She had other, less obvious, powers too.

The little moonstone necklace she had been given on the day she was born reflected her moods. Now, as she ran, it was glowing pure white beneath her jumper. Jaws, flying above her head, was aware of it, and that made him happy too. He looped a loop, then swooped down to ride on Lottie's shoulder.

Twenty minutes later, Lottie and Jaws reached the gates of Shadow Academy.

'Oh, dear . . .' Lottie was wide-eyed as she looked at the huge grey stone building in front of her. 'I do hope it's going to be all right. What do you think, Jaws?'

Jaws fluttered round her head. '*Eeeek*,' he squeaked. '*Eeeek!*'

'You're right.' Lottie took a firmer hold of her school bag. 'I'm Lottie Luna and I'm not scared of anything!' And with her head held high, she marched up the steps and in through the wide-open front door.

Find out what happens next in
***Lottie Luna and the Bloom Garden*!**